Young Lions

Salford Road
and other poems

Other books by Gareth Owen

Song of the City
Douglas the Drummer

for older readers

Never Walk Alone
The Man With Eyes Like Windows

Gareth Owen

Salford Road
and other poems

Illustrated by Alan Marks

Young Lions
An Imprint of HarperCollins Publishers

for Hilary

Poems 1–30 and 41 first published under the title *Salford Road*
by Kestrel Books 1979
This collection under the title *Salford Road and other poems*
first published in Young Lions 1988
Fifth impression July 1992

Young Lions is an imprint of the Children's Division,
part of HarperCollins Publishers Ltd,
77–85 Fulham Palace Road, Hammersmith,
London W6 8JB

Printed and bound in Great Britain by
HarperCollins Manufacturing, Glasgow

Acknowledgements
'Our School', 'Denis Law', 'The Fight', 'Winter Days', Ping-
Pong' first published in *Wordscapes* by Oxford University Press
1971; 'Bedroom Skating', 'Drama Lesson', 'Uncle Alfred's Long
Jump', 'The Ghoul', 'Den to Let' first published in *Bright Lights
Blaze Out* by Oxford University Press 1986; 'Dear Examiner'
first published in *Schools Out* by Oxford University Press 1987.
'Street Boy' first published in *Young Winter's Tales 5* by
Macmillan London Ltd 1974.

Contents

Cycling down the street
to meet my friend John

On my bike and down our street,
Swinging round the bend,
Whizzing past the Library,
Going to meet my friend.

Silver flash of spinning spokes,
Whirr of oily chain,
Bump of tyre on railway line
Just before the train.

The road bends sharp at Pinfold Lane
Like a broken arm,
Brush the branches of the trees
Skirting Batty's Farm.

Tread and gasp and strain and bend
Climbing Gallows' Slope,
Flying down the other side
Like an antelope.

Swanking into Johnnie's street,
Cycling hands on hips,
Past O'Connors corner shop
That always smells of chips.

Bump the door of his backyard
Where we always play,
Lean my bike and knock the door,
"Can John come out to play?"

Going to the Dentist

After tea
Trev and me
Have to go up to Whinnick
And visit the clinic
To have our teeth looked at. My mum makes me go
every month. I think that's overdoing things but
there's no arguing with her.

We sit down
Look around
There are three in the queue
We both say, "After you",
At exactly the same moment but in the end I know
it's going to be me that goes in first. Always is. Still,
there's something to be said for getting it over with.

I spend an age
Reading the Sporting Page
Trev shuffles on his seat
and swings his nervous feet
About all over the place trying to look right casual
but I know all the time that inside he's as scared as
I am.

An old man blows
His old man's nose;
Clock strikes six.
Bite nails, count the ticks
But time doesn't half drag. Perhaps we're too late.

Perhaps he won't have time to see us. After I've
counted a hundred he'll come out looking sad and tell
us to go home. But he doesn't.

A baby cries
A mother sighs
And lifts her on her knee.
Wonder what he'll do to me?
Please don't let him take any out. Or give me gas. I
can't stand gas. Anything but gas. Anything that is
except the needle. Or the drill anything except the
drill. I want to go home.

Or a filling
Can be killing.
Cough, look without a care
But inside I say a prayer
Promising to clean my teeth three times a day and
four times on Sunday until the day I die as long as he
doesn't do any fillings or take any out and there's no
gas or injections. Another thing about this dentist
they say he used to be an SS officer but I'm not sure if
there's much truth in that.

Only Trev and me
For the dentist to see.
I wonder staring at the wall
Why we have any teeth at all
I'm sure we could get along without them. I wouldn't
mind living on milk and mashed potato or even
sucking everything through a straw.

The dentist looks at me.
"Open wide, let me see."
Tongue's huge, throat dry
But I heave a sigh
Of relief when he says my teeth are all right and I
don't have to come back for another three months.
Funny how I forget all the promises I've made.

Trev tries to grin
As he goes in.
"What's he like? Did he take any out? What did he
do?"
"Oh, he filled a few, took out one or two, there's
nothing to it at all."
And I clap him on the back as he goes past. He looks
very white suddenly. I put my hands in my pockets
and look out of the window. Traffic rumbles by. Sun
shines. Wonder what we'll have for supper?

My Dog Robbo

Mongrel dog Robbo up got,
Thumped 'is ol' tail
What's tied up loose like an undone granny
And wagger-wagged it quite a lot.

Mongrel body on four sticks,
Mongrel napper full of tricks,
Mongrel pelt stuffed with tics,
Mongrel gob wet of licks.

Scraps out, sups all,
Nabs all eyes light on,
Scoffs tin tacks and half bricks,
Chews all teeth bite on.

Knocks the purr out of pussies,
Fights the legs on our bed,
Woofs the wind up red buses
And leaves them for dead.

Howl like a squeaky brake,
Stink like a bog,
You get under the world's skin
That's Robbo my dog.

Salford Road

Salford Road, Salford Road,
Is the place where I was born,
With a green front gate, a red brick wall
And hydrangeas round a lawn.

Salford Road, Salford Road,
Is the road where we would play
Where the sky lay over the roof tops
Like a friend who'd come to stay.

The Gardeners lived at fifty-five,
The Lunds with the willow tree,
Mr Pool with the flag and the garden pond
And the Harndens at fifty-three.

There was riding bikes and laughing
Till we couldn't laugh any more,
And bilberries picked on the hillside
And picnics on the shore.

I lay in bed when I was four
As the sunlight turned to grey
And heard the train through my pillow
And the seagulls far away.

And I rose to look out of my window
For I knew that someone was there
And a man stood as sad as nevermore
And didn't see me there.

And when I stand in Salford Road
And think of the boy who was me
I feel that from one of the windows
Someone is looking at me.

My friends walked out one Summer day,
Walked singing down the lane,
My friends walked into a wood called Time
And never came out again.

We live in a land called Gone-Today
That's made of bricks and straw
But Salford Road runs through my head
To a land called Evermore.

Sports Report

Five o'clock of a Saturday night,
November out of doors,
We sit down to tea,
My family and me,
To hear the football scores.

I'm the one in our family who tries to listen but
everyone else just talks and talks and talks.

Dad discusses his rose trees,
Stephen chokes on his bread,
Grandad moans
About the cold in his bones
And talks about people who're dead.

Betty dreams about Terry,
"Who's handsome and ever so tall."
When Mum joins in
There's such a din
You can't hear the scores at all.

Well a few, but the worst is only hearing half a result,
that's very frustrating that is.

Did Fulham win at Fratton Park?
Did Millwall lose at the Den?
What happend to Blackpool at Boothferry Park?
Did Doncaster draw again?

Who dropped a point at Derby?
A fight in the crowd at where?
"There's a terrible draught,
I'm freezing to death
And nobody seems to care."

Who was sent off at Southampton?
Who was booked at West Ham?
"I'm pleased with that rose."
"Stop picking your nose."
"Will somebody pass me the jam."

The Owls beat the Blades in a derby,
Cardiff beat Carlisle three–nil.
"He looks ever so young
With his hair all long."
"Will someone fetch Grandad his pill."

Someone lost at the Valley,
The Orient somehow got four.
"You're not to eat jam
With your fingers young man,
You get the knife from the drawer."

Plymouth Argyle whipped Walsall,
Darlington managed a draw.
"Our Betty, stop dreamin'
And look after Stephen,
He's pouring the sauce on the floor."

Wrexham romped home at The Racecourse,
The Sandgrounders' winger got three.
"With a touch of compost
And some luck with the frost
We might get some blooms on that tree."

I've missed Albion and City and Chelsea,
Queens Park and Chester and Crewe.
"Get your grandad his scarf,
There's no need to laugh
We don't want him dying of flu."

A sudden reversal at Reading,
A last minute winner at York.
"Turn down that radio!
D'you hear what I say to you
I can hardly hear myself talk."

Yes, but you wait till she wants to listen to
something,
I'm not even allowed to breathe. Just to be awkward
everybody goes quiet when the Scottish results come
on.

Those strange-sounding teams up in Scotland,
Kilmarnock and Brechin and Clyde,
And players with names like Macintosh,
MacDonald, McNab and MacBride.

Who wants to know about Berwick
Or Forfar, Stranraer and Dundee,
That Hibernian were humbled at Hampden,
That Stirling slammed Celtic eight-three?

The only thing left to do is to go and get the paper.
Trouble is I haven't any money left.

Mum starts clearing the table,
Stacking the plates in the sink.
Would Dad think it funny
If I borrowed some money
To buy the *Sporting Pink*?

While Mum's out of the room he slips me five pence.
I'll have to pay him back of course. He's very strict
about things like that, my dad.

I race through the fog up to Jackson's,
Pumping out breath like steam.
I've got to find out
How United made out
They're my favourite team.

So I run my finger down the list of scores looking
for the result.

United, United, United.
Never mind about the rest.
They've won, they've won,
Like they ought to have done,
Through a last minute header from Best.

When your team wins everything's all right.

I shuffle through leaves in the gutter,
Whistle a tune through my teeth,
Tightrope on walls,
Head imaginary balls,
My family's not bad underneath.

Winter

On Winter mornings in the playground
The boys stand huddled,
Their cold hands doubled
Into trouser pockets.
The air hangs frozen
About the buildings
And the cold is an ache in the blood
And a pain on the tender skin
Beneath finger nails.
The odd shouts
Sound off like struck iron
And the sun
Balances white
Above the boundary wall.
I fumble my bus ticket
Between numb fingers
Into a fag,
Take a drag
And blow white smoke
Into the December air.

Our School

I go to Weld Park Primary,
It's near the Underpass
And five blocks past the Cemetery
And two roads past the Gas
Works with the big tower that smells so bad
    me and me mates put our hankies over our
        faces and pretend we're being attacked
            by poison gas . . . and that.

There's this playground with lines for rounders,
And cricket stumps chalked on the wall,
And kids with their coats for goalposts
Booting a tennis ball
Around all over the place and shoutin' and arguin'
    about offside and they always kick it over
        the garden wall next door and she
            goes potty and tells our head teacher
          and he gets right ratty with
              everybody and stops us playin'
               football . . .
                  . . . and everything.

We have this rule at our school
You've to wait till the whistle blows
And you can't go in till you hear it
Not even if it snows.

And your wellies get filled with water and your socks
   go all soggy and start slipping down your legs
      and your hands get so cold they go all
         crumpled and you can't undo
            the buttons of your mac when
               you do get inside . . .
                  . . . it's true.

The best thing is our classroom.
When it's fine you can see right far,
Past the Catholic Cathedral
Right to the Morris Car
Works where me dad works as a fitter and sets off
   right early every morning in these overalls
      with his snap in this sandwich box and
         a flask of tea and always moanin'
            about the money . . . honest.

In Hall we pray for brotherly love
And sing hymns that are ever so long
And the Head shouts at Linda Nutter
Who's always doing wrong.
She can't keep out of trouble because
   she's always talkin'
      she can't stop our teacher says she
         must have been injected with
            a gramophone needle she talks
               so much and
that made me laugh once
not any more though I've heard it
   too often . . . teachers!

Loving your enemy sounds all right
Until you open your eyes
And you're standing next to Nolan
Who's always telling lies
About me and getting me into trouble and about
   three times a week I fight him after school
      it's like a habit I've got
         but I can't love him even though
            I screw my eyes up real hard and try like
              mad, but if it wasn't him it
                would be somebody else
                I mean
                    you've got to have enemies . . .
                    . . . haven't you?

We sing "O to be a pilgrim"
And think about God and heaven
And then we're told the football team lost
By thirteen goals to seven
But that's not bad because St Xavier's don't half have
   big lads in their team and last time we played
      they beat us eighteen one and this time
         we got seven goals . . .
            . . . didn't we?

Then we have our lessons,
We have Science and English and Maths,
Except on Wednesday morning
When our class goes to the baths

And it's not half cold and Peter Bradberry's
   fingers went all wrinkled and blue last week
    and I said, "You're goin' to die, man"
       but he pushed me under the water and I had to
       hold my breath for fifteen minutes.
          But he's still alive though . . .
             . . . he is.

Friday's my favourite day though,
We have Art all afternoon
And I never care what happens
Cos I know it's home-time soon
And I'm free for two whole days but I think
   sometimes it wouldn't be half so good
     having this weekend if we didn't have five
      days
        of
           school
             in
               between—
Would it?

Sharon's Life

My name is Sharon
I have two brothers
Called Phillip and William
Sometimes they bother me
But often they don't.
Being me is fun.
When it is older
It won't be so good I think.
Phillip lost my book
It had pictures
He lost it
But I am not very cross.
Daddy bought it.
Aunt Judy died last week
Mummy said it was a loss
And then she cried
Quite a bit.
My dog is called Spot
He has some bad habits.
Perhaps I will find the book.
My bed is green.
I'm five.
That's all.
I'm glad I'm alive.

The Cat

When the moon is leering yellow
And the trees are witches' claws
That scratch upon the window panes
And scrape upon the doors,
I crouch before the fireplace
And smirk into the heat
And think of wild adventures
That are waiting up the street –
But I'm tooooo tiiiiired.

I could slink along the alleyway
That's sentinelled with bins
And nose inside old papers
And lick the empty tins.
I could sniff out mice in the Railway Yard
Or watch the Midnight Mail
Thunder through the station
Rattling his angry tail –
But I'm tooooo laaaaazy.

I could tease the dogs in the school-yard
Pretending they're not there
And swagger in front of their noses
With my head up in the air
And when they start to chase me
And howl and tumble and call
I'd nimbly leap from their snapping jaws
And smile at them from the wall –
But I'm tooooo sleeeeepy.

I could go and meet the tabby
Who only comes out at night
And the rather belligerent ginger
Who lost his ear in a fight.
I'll howl, I'll miaowl by the lamppost,
I'll race, I'll roister, I'll roam,
I'll wander the night by the moon's yellow light
I'll never want to go home . . .
Tomoooooroooooow.

Saturdays

Real
Genuine
Saturdays
Like marbles
Conkers
Sweet new potatoes
Have their especial season
Are all morning
With midday at five o'clock.
True Saturdays
Are borrowed from early Winter
And the left overs
Of Autumn sunshine days
But separate from days of snow.
The skies dine on dwindles of smoke
Where leafy plots smoulder
With small fires.
Sunday meat is bought
And late
Large, white loaves
From little corner shops.
People passing
Wave over garden walls,
Greengrocers and milkmen are smiled upon
And duly paid.
It is time for the chequered tablecloth
And bowls of soup.

And early on
We set out with some purpose
Through only
Lovely Saturday,
Under skies
Like sun-shot water,
For the leccy train
And the Match in Liverpool.

Denis Law

I live at 14 Stanhope Street,
Me mum, me dad and me,
And three of us have made a gang,
John Stokes and Trev and me.

Our favourite day is Saturday;
We go Old Trafford way
And wear red colours in our coats
To watch United play.

We always stand behind the goal
In the middle of the roar.
The others come to see the game –
I come for Denis Law.

His red sleeves flap around his wrists,
He's built all thin and raw,
But the toughest backs don't stand a chance
When the ball's near Denis Law.

He's a whiplash when he's in control,
He can swivel like an eel,
And twist and sprint in such a way
It makes defences reel.

And when he's hurtling for the goal
I know he's got to score.
Defences may stop normal men –
They can't stop Denis Law.

We all race home when full time blows
To kick a tennis ball,
And Trafford Park is our back-yard,
And the stand is next door's wall.

Old Stokesey shouts, "I'm Jimmy Greaves,"
And scores against the door,
And Trev shouts: "I'll be Charlton," –
But I am Denis Law.

Boredom

Boredom
Is
Me
Gloomy as Monday
Moidering the time away
Murdering the holiday
Just
Sort of waiting.

Boredom
Is
Clouds
Black as old slate
Chucking rain straight
On our Housing Estate
All grey
Day long.

Boredom
Is
John
In bed again
The trickle of rain
On the window pane
And no one
To play with.

Boredom
Is
Trev
Gone for the day

To Colwyn Bay
For a holiday
And me
On my own.

Boredom
Is
My comics all read
The Library closed
Damp clothes before the fire
Deciding
Not to clean my bike
To tidy my room
To help with washing

Boredom
Is
Empty streets
And black telegraph poles
A muddy tractor
On the building site
Shipwrecked in mud

Boredom
Is
A thick circle
Of emptiness
Heaviness
Nothingness
With me
Slumped in the middle

Boredom
Is
Boredom
Boredom is
Boredom
Is
Boredom
Boredom is
Boredom
Is
Boredom
Boredom is
Boredom
Is
Boredom
Boredom is
Boredom
Is
Boredom
Boredom is
Boredom
Is
Boredom
Boredom is
Boredom
Is
Boredom
Boredom is
Boredom
Is
Boredom
Boredom is
Boredom
Is

Jonah and the Whale

Well, to start with
It was dark
So dark
You couldn't see
Your hand in front of your face;
And huge
Huge as an acre of farmland.
How do I know?
Well, I paced it out
Length and breadth
That's how.
And if you was to shout
You'd hear your own voice resound,
Bouncing along the ridges of its stomach,
Like when you call out
Under a bridge
Or in an empty hall.
Hear anything?
No not much,
Only the normal
Kind of sounds
You'd expect to hear
Inside a whale's stomach;
The sea swishing far away,
Food gurgling, the wind
and suchlike sounds;
Then there was me screaming for help,
But who'd be likely to hear,
Us being miles from
Any shipping lines

And anyway
Supposing someone did hear,
Who'd think of looking inside a whale?
That's not the sort of thing
That people do.
Smell? I'll say there was a smell.
And cold. The wind blew in
Something terrible from the South
Each time he opened his mouth
Or took a swallow of some tit bit.
The only way I found
To keep alive at all
Was to wrap my arms
Tight around myself
And race from wall to wall.

Damp? You can say that again;
When the ocean came sluicing in
I had to climb his ribs
To save myself from drowning.
Fibs? You think I'm telling you fibs,
I haven't told the half of it brother.
I'm only giving a modest account
Of what these two eyes have seen
And that's the truth on it.
Here, one thing I'll say
Before I'm done –
Catch me eating fish
From now on.

This and That

Two cats together
In bee–heavy weather
After the August day
In smug contentment lay
By the garden shed
In the flower bed
Yawning out the hours
In the shade of the flowers
And passed the time away,
Between stretching and washing and sleeping,
Talking over the day.

"Climbed a tree."
"Aaaah."
"Terrorised sparrows."
"Mmmmh."
"Was chased."
"Aaaah."
"Fawned somewhat!"
"Mmmmh."
"Washed, this and that,"
Said the first cat.

And they passed the time away
Between stretching and washing and sleeping
Talking over the day.

"Gazed out of parlour window."
"Aaaah."
"Pursued blue bottles."
"Mmmmh."
"Clawed curtains."
"Aaaah."
"Was cuffed."
"Mmmmh."
"Washed, this and that."
Said the other cat.

And they passed the time away
Between stretching and washing and sleeping
Talking over the day.

"Scratched to be let in."
"Aaaah."
"Patrolled the house."
"Mmmmh."
"Scratched to go out."
"Aaaah."
"Was booted."
"Mmmmh."
"Washed, this and that."
Said the first cat.

And they passed the time away
Between stretching and washing and sleeping
Talking over the day.

"Lapped cream elegantly."
"Aaaah."
"Disdained dinner."
"Mmmmh,"
"Borrowed a little salmon."
"Aaaah."
"Was tormented."
"Mmmmh."
"Washed, this and that."
Said the other cat.

And they passed the time away
Between stretching and washing and sleeping
Talking over the day.

"Chased a shadow or two."
"Aaaah."
"Met friends."
"Mmmmh."
"Sang a little."
"Aaaah."
"Avoided water."
"Mmmmh."
"Washed, this and that."
Said the first cat.

And they passed the time away
Between stretching and washing and sleeping
Talking over the day.

Photograph

Is that you and is that me
Captured by photography?
Is that Auntie, is that Dad?
Is that face the face I had?

Are those clothes the clothes I wore?
Are those skies the skies I saw?
Those the hills that round me ranged?
Is it me or they have changed?

Did Auntie Gwladys wear that hat?
What made Beryl smile like that?
Why is Eileen staring right?
What was happening out of sight?

What the dreams that filled our heads?
What the words that once were said?
What would he I used to be
If he met me think of me.

Real Life

"Yes," thought John
his eyes gleaming with excitement
as he looked round the ancient Inn
on the edge of the moors
that was connected to
otherwise inaccessible St Peter's Cove
which had once been a haunt of smugglers
by a secret underground passage
from his bedroom
and which his strange Aunt Lucy
had rented to his mother and father
and Uncle David for
the whole summer holidays.
"Yes, this looks just the sort
of place for an adventure but
that kind of thing
only happens in books."
And he was right.

Ping-Pong

Swatted between bats
The celluloid ball
Leaps on unseen elastic
Skimming the taut net

Sliced		Spun
Screwed		Cut
Dabbed		Smashed
	Point	
	Service	
Ping		Pong
Pong		Ping
Bing		Bong
Bong		Bing
	Point	
	Service	
Ding		Dong
Dong		Ding
Ting		Tong
Tang		Tong
	Point	
	Service	
Angled		Slipped
Cut		Driven
Floated		Caressed
Driven		Hammered
	THWACKED	
	Point	
	Service	

Bit		Bat
Tip		Tap
Slip		Slap
Zip		Zap
Whip		Whap
	Point	
	Service	
Left		Yes
Right		Yes
Twist		Yes
Skids		Yes
Eighteen		Seventeen
Eighteen		All
Nineteen		Eighteen
Nineteen		All
Twenty		Nineteen
	Point	
	Service	
Forehand		Backhand
Swerves		Yes
Rockets·		Yes
Battered		Ah
Cracked		Ah

SMASHED

SMASHED

SMASHED

GAME

The Stomach Ache

Somebody is in there
Where I can't reach,
Somebody with a grudge
And a knowledge of torture,
Some evil thing
Who sups on suffering,
Someone whose yellow fingers
Knead and plunge,
Someone who smiles
And while he smiles
Screws up my innards
In malicious knots,
Someone with eyes tight closed
And wrinkles on his flesh,
Someone who pummels with his bony elbows,
Gurgles with green glee
And stamps his boots about
And starts to suck me
Through his broken teeth
Swallowing me, inside out.

Sitting on Trev's back wall on the last day of the holidays trying to think of something to do

We sit and squint on Trev's back wall
By the clothes line
Watching the shirts flap
Hearing the shirts slap
In the sunshine.
There's nothing much to do at all
But try to keep cool
And it's our last day
Of the holiday
Tomorrow we're back at school.

We keep suggesting games to play
Like Monopoly,
But you need a day
If you want to play
It properly.
We played for four hours yesterday
Between rainfalls
In Trev's front room
That's like a tomb
And always smells of mothballs.

Says Trev, "Why don't we kick a ball
Over the Wasteground?"
But the weather's got
Far too hot
To run around.

John kicks his heels against the wall
Stokesey scratches his head
I head a ball
Chalk my name on the wall
While Trev pretends that he's dead.

Says John, "Let's go to the cinder track
And play speedway.
We can go by the dykes
It's not far on our bikes
I'll lead the way."
"My saddlebag's all straw at the back
Being used by blackbirds."
"And there's something unreal
About my fixed wheel
It only drives me backwards."

Trev's Granny chucks out crusts of bread
For the sparrows
While their black cat
Crouches flat
Winking in the shadows.
Trev leaps up and bangs his head
With a sudden roar.
"We could er. . . . .," he says.
"We could er. . . . .," he says.
And then sits down once more..

"Let's play Releevo on the sands,"
Says John at last.
We set out with a shout
But his mother calls out,
"It's gone half past
Your tea's all laid, you wash your hands
They're absolutely grey."
"Oh go on Mum
Do I have to come
We were just going out to play."

Old Stokes trails home and pulls a face,
"I'll see you Trev."
"See you John."
"See you Trev."
"See you tonight the usual place."
"Yes right, all right."
"Don't forget."
"You bet."
"See you then tonight."
"See you."
"See you."
"See
You."

Empty House

There is nothing
Quite so dismal
As an empty house;
The door bell's clangour
Tears apart the silence
Rousing no one.
Nothing moves;
Not a sound
Save the chasing echoes
And the clock's hollow
Tock, tock
Measuring the emptiness;
Behind the frosted door
No friendly, welcome shadow looms,
No footsteps cross the floor.

The yellow key
Hides coldly in its hiding place
Behind the rusty carcass of the B.S.A.
Amongst old tins of paint;
Maps of oil stain the floor
And in the air the smell
Of dust and turps and sawdust
(Property of all garages).
Whistling softly,
I turn the key
And open the door slowly,
As if the emptiness
Was a stranger
I might find sitting
Silent in an armchair.

The house is strange,
Not mine any more,
Holding its breath,
Waiting; a house not real,
Not itself
But an accurate copy taken from life,
Familiar but lacking warmth.
The note from mother
Telling me not to let the fire go out
Scrawled on an envelope
Leans against the clock.
I wander through deserted rooms
Touching familiar objects;
Comforted by companionable flowers in a jar
And by the bulk of our white cat
Who dozes on whatever.

The coals have crumbled to ash;
The fire is out.
I lie, my feet up on a chair,
Reading my comic,
Wishing my mother could be home
To tell me not to put them there.

Unemployable

"I usth thu workth in the thircusth,"
He said,
Between the intermittent showers that
emerged from his mouth.
"Oh," I said, "what did you do?"
"I usth thu catcth bulleth in my theeth."

The Fight

The kick off is
I don't like him;
Nothing about him.
He's fat and soft;
Like a jellybaby he is.
Now he's never done nothing,
Not to me,
He wouldn't dare:
Nothing at all of anything like that.
I just can't stand him,
So I'll fight him
And I'll beat him,
I could beat him any day.

The kick off is it's his knees:
They knock together,
They sock together.
And they're fat,
With veins that run into his socks
Too high.
Like a girl he is,
And his shorts,
Too long,
They look
All wrong,
Like a Mum's boy.
Then
He simpers and dimples,
Like a big lass he is;

So I'll fight him
Everyone beats him,
I could beat him any day.

For another thing it's his hair,
All smarmed and oily fair,
All silk and parted flat,
His mum does it like that
With her flat hand and water,
All licked and spittled into place,
With the quiff all down his face.
And his satchel's new
With his name in blue
Chalked on it.
So I chalked on it,
"Trevor is a cissie"
On it.
So he's going to fight me,
But I'll beat him,
I could beat him any day.

There's a crowd behind the sheds
When we come they turn their heads
Shouting and laughing,
Wanting blood and a bashing.
Take off my coat, rush him,
Smash him, bash him
Lash him, crash him
In the head,
In the bread
Basket.

Crack, thwack,
He's hit me back
Shout and scream
"Gerroff me back,
Gerroff, gerroff!
You wait, I'll get you,
I could beat you any day!"

Swing punch, bit his hand.
Blood on teeth, blood on sand.
Buttons tear, shouts and sighs,
Running nose, tears in eyes.

I'll get him yet; smack him yet.
Smash his smile, teacher's pet.
Brow grazed by knuckle
Knees begin to buckle.
"Gerroff me arms you're hurtin' me!"
"Give in?"
"No."
"Give in?"
"No. Gerroff me arms!"
"Give in?"
"No."
"Give in?"
"GIVE IN?"
"NEVER."
"GIVE IN?"
"OOOH GERROFF GERROFF."
"GIVE IN?"
"I. . . give . . . in . . . yeah."

Don't cry, don't cry,
Wipe tears from your eye.
Walk home all alone
In the gutters all alone.
Next time I'll send him flying,
I wasn't really trying;
I could beat him any day.

Winter Days

Biting air
Winds blow
City streets
Under snow

Noses red
Lips sore
Runny eyes
Hands raw

Chimneys smoke
Cars crawl
Piled snow
On garden wall

Slush in gutters
Ice in lanes
Frosty patterns
On window panes

Morning call
Lift up head
Nipped by winter
Stay in bed

Friday Morning Last Two Lessons
is Games Day

We straggle in twos
Down Endbutt Lane to the playing fields,
In a gap-toothed murmuring line
Filling the pavement.
Mr Pearson strides out in front
The ball tucked firmly under one arm,
His head bent.

We avoid lampposts
And young mothers pushing prams,
Sometimes walk gammy-legged in gutters
Or scuffle through damp leaves.
The morning is filled
With laughter-tongued and pottering mongrels;
Old men tending bare borders
Slowly unbend
And lean upon their brooms to watch us pass.
Their wives in flowered pinnies
Peer through the lace curtains
Of unused front rooms.

At the pitch
We change in the old pavilion
That smells of dust and feet
And has knot holes in the boarding.

Someone
From another class
Has left
One
Blue and white sock behind.
The lads shout about other games
And goals and saves and shots
Or row about who'll wear red or blue.
Pearson blows exasperation
Briskly through his whistle,
"Come on lads, let's be having you."

With eighteen a side
We tear after the ball shouting,
Longing to give it a good clean belt,
Perform some piece of perfection –
Beat three sprawling backs in a mazy dribble,
Race full pelt onto a plate-laid-on pass
And crack it full of hate and zest
Past the diving goalie to bulge the net.
But there is no net
And we have to leg it after the ball
To the allotments by the lane
Before we can take centre
To start the game again.

Afterwards,
Still wearing football socks,
Studded boots slung on my shoulder,
I say "Tarrah" to Trev
At Station Road and drift home
Playing the game again.
Smoke climbs steep from neat red chimneys;
Babies drool and doze
And laugh at the empty sky.
There is the savour of cabbage and gravy
About the Estate and the flowers do not hear
The great crowd roaring me on.

Street Boy

Just you look at me, man,
Stompin' down the street
My crombie stuffed with biceps
My boots is filled with feet.

Just you hark to me, man,
When they call us out
My head is full of silence
My mouth is full of shout.

Just you watch me move, man,
Steady like a clock
My heart is spaced on blue beat
My soul is stoned on rock.

Just you read my name, man,
Writ for all to see
The walls is red with stories
The streets is filled with me.

Friends

When first I went to school
I walked with Sally.
She carried my lunch pack,
Told me about a book she'd read
With a handsome hero
So I said,
"You be my best friend."
After break I went right off her.
I can't say why
And anyway I met Joan
Who's pretty with dark curls
And we sat in a corner of the playground
And giggled about the boy who brought the milk.
Joan upset me at lunch,
I can't remember what she said actually,
But I was definitely upset
And took up with Hilary
Who's frightfully brilliant and everything
And showed me her history
Which I considered very decent.
The trouble with Hilary is
She has to let you know how clever she is
And I said,
"You're not the only one who's clever you know,"
And she went all quiet and funny
And hasn't spoken to me since.
Good riddance I say
And anyway Linda is much more my type of girl;
She does my hair in plaits
And says how pretty I look,

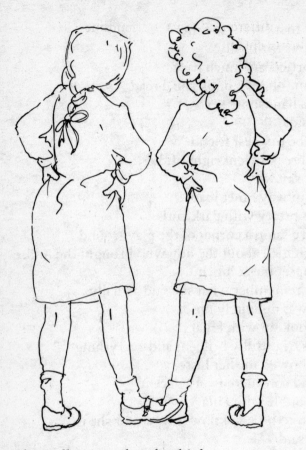

She really says what she thinks
And I appreciate that.
Nadine said she was common
When we saw her on the bus that time
Sitting with three boys from that other school,
And I had to agree
There was something in what she said.

There's a difference between friendliness
And being cheap
And I thought it my duty
To tell her what I thought.
Well she laughed right in my face
And then pretended I wasn't there
So I went right off her.
If there's one thing I can't stand
It's being ignored and laughed at.
Nadine understood what I meant,
Understood right away
And that's jolly nice in a friend.
I must tell you one thing about her,
She's rather a snob.
I get the feeling
She looks down on me
And she'll never come to my house
Though I've asked her thousands of times.
I thought it best to have it out with her
And she went off in a huff
Which rather proved my point
And I considered myself well rid.

At the moment
I walk home on my own
But I'm keeping my eyes open
And when I see somebody I consider suitable
I'll befriend her.

Moggy in the City

Old fat moggy
Padding on grimy cobbles
Slouching past washing
Rooting in dustbins
Picking your way past puddles
Gliding down ginnels
Miaowling on walls
Purring and rubbing
Round mothers and prams
Rambling through rubbish heaps
Crouching in old cars
Treading the streets
Of dirty old Mother Liverpool.
You,
I feel,
Deserved more
But you betray no resentment
In slow-closing eyes
And somehow with stripes
And regal softness
Make our city better.

A Stomach Ache is Worse Away from Home

"Sir," I said,
Hoping for sympathy,
"I've got the stomach ache,"
All of it was true,
There was no putting it on.
I gave out winces with my mouth
Using my eyebrows skilfully
And held the hurt place hard
With both hands.
But it was my white face convinced him.
So he sent me outside
To walk it away in the fresh air.
Outside it was deathly cold.
Because he had his hand up first
Trev came out too
To see I was all right.
A grey wind with rain in it
Whipped across the playground,
Spattering through puddles
And setting the empties rolling
Up and down, up and down
And clatter-rattling in their crates.
Trev said, "You'll be all right."
And started kicking a tennis ball
Up against the toilet wall,
His hands in his pockets,
Bent against the cold.
The dinner ladies came out.
Moaning slightly I bent over
And gritted my teeth bravely.

But they didn't see
And walked through the school gates laughing.
At home there would be the smell of cooking
And our Robbo asleep before the fire.
I looked through the railings
And thought my way to our house.
Past the crumbling wall,
The Bingo Hall,
The scraggy tree
As thin as me,
The rotting boarding
By the cinema
With last week's star
In a Yankee car
Flapping on the hoarding.
Stop!
Turn right towards town
And three doors down,
That's our house.

The Wind

Listen to the wind awailing
Rattling the garden gate
Brushing the leaves of the oak tree
Rustling in the grate.

The cat lies flat on the hearth rug
Washing his face with his paws
The dog's asleep in the basket
Everyone's indoors.

It screams along the alleys
It bellows up the street
It groans between the gravestones
It bowls hats along the street.

It's pounding at the windows
Like the hooves of an angry horse
If it blows like this much longer
It'll knock the world off its course.

It's quietened down at bedtime
Snoring loud and deep
At six it rattles the milk crates
And finally falls asleep.

Hymn to the Twentieth Century

Give me a new Ford car around me,
Four Goodyear tyres below,
And Belsize undersealing
To protect me from the snow.

Give me High Speed Gas to warm me,
And Slumbertight by night,
Venetian blinds by Windofurn
To filter in the light.

Let the telly be my window
On all that lives without,
And my Dina pop transistor
Beat the silence out.

Give me beef steaks made in factories,
Potatoes grown in tins,
Let the Welfare State that loves me
Expiate my sins.

Let my shirt be made of Nusilk,
That cost the worm no sleep,
And the pile on my Woolies' sweater
Be clipped from synthetic sheep.

The plastic flowers in my garden
Have a brightness that can't be ignored,
And the lawn just never needs cutting
When it's sown by Cyril Lord.

Don't kick the second millennium,
Don't let it make you feel low,
Just make the best of what you've got,
There's nowhere else you can go.

Bedroom Skating

Because there is no Ice Rink
Within fifty miles of our house,
My sister perfects her dance routines
In the Olympic Stadium of my bedroom.
Wearing a soft expression
And two big, yellow dusters on her feet,
She explodes out of cupboards
To an avalanche of music
And whirls about the polished lino
In a blur of double axels and triple salchows.
For her free-style doubles
She hurls this pillow called Torvill
From here to breakfast-time
While spinning like a hippo
Round and round my bed.
Imagine waking up to that each morning;
Small wonder my hands shake
And I'm off my cornflakes.

Last Thursday she even made me
Stand up on my bed
And hold up cards marked "Six"
While she gave victory salutes
In the direction of the gerbil's cage.
To be honest,
Despite her endless dedication
And her hours of practice
I don't think she has a hope
Of lifting the world title.
But who cares?
She may not get the gold
But I'll bet there isn't another skater alive
With wall-to-wall mirror
On her bedroom floor.

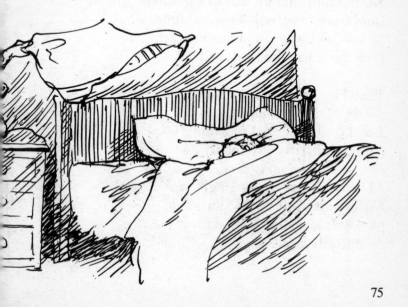

Drama Lesson

"Let's see some super shapes you Blue Group,"
Mr Lavender shouts down the hall.
"And forests don't forget your trembly leaves
And stand up straight and tall."

But Phillip Chubb is in our group
And he wants to be Robin Hood
And Ann Boot is sulking because she's not with
her friend
And I don't see why I should be wood.

The lights are switched on in the classrooms,
Outside the sky's nearly black,
And the dining-hall smells of gravy and fat
And Chubb has boils down his back.

Sir tells him straight that he's got to be tree
But he won't wave his arms around.
"How can I wave my branches, Sir,
Friar Tuck has chopped them all down."

Then I come cantering through Sherwood
To set Maid Marion free
And I really believe I'm Robin Hood
And the Sheriff's my enemy.

At my back my trusty longbow
My broadsword clanks at my side,
My outlaws gallop behind me
As into adventure we ride.

"Untie that maid you villain," I shout
With all the strength I have,
But the tree has got bored and is picking his nose
And Maid Marion has gone to the lav.

After rehearsals, Sir calls us together
And each group performs their play,
But just as it comes to our turn
The bell goes for the end of the day.

As I trudge my way home through the city streets
The cars and the houses retreat
And a thunder of hooves beats in my mind
And I gallop through acres of wheat.

The castle gleams white in the distance,
The banners flap, golden and red,
And distant trumpets weave silver dreams
In the landscape of my head.

Uncle Alfred's Long Jump

When Mary Rand
Won the Olympic Long Jump,
My Auntie Hilda
Paced out the distance
On the pavement outside her house.
"Look at that!"
She shouted challengingly
At the dustman, the milkman, the grocer,
Two Jehovah's Witnesses
And a male St Bernard
Who happened to be passing,
"A girl, a girl did that;
If you men are so clever
Let's see what you can do."
Nobody took up the challenge
Until Uncle Alfred trudged home
Tired from the office
Asking for his tea.
"Our Mary did that!"
Said Auntie Hilda proudly
Pointing from the lamppost
To the rose bush by her gate.
"You men are so clever,
Let's see how near
That rose bush you end up."
His honour and manhood at stake,
Uncle Alfred put down his bowler
His briefcase and his brolly
And launched himself
Into a fifty yard run-up.

"End up at that rose bush,"
He puffed mockingly,
"I'll show you where I'll end up."
His take-off from the lamppost
Was a thing of beauty,
But where he ended up
Was in The Royal Infirmary
With both legs in plaster.
"Some kind of record!"
He said proudly to the bone specialist;
While through long nights
In a ward full of coughs and snoring
He dreamed about the washing line
And of how to improve
His high jump technique.

The Ghoul

One dark and wintry evening
When snow swirled through the air
And the wind howled like a banshee
I crept silently up the stair.

I sat in the quiet of my bedroom
And opened with bated breath
My "Zombie Horror Make-Up Kit"
That would frighten my sister to death.

"FRIGHTEN YOUR FAMILY! AMAZE YOUR
   FRIENDS!
With our do-it-yourself make-up kits.
BE A WEREWOLF! A VAMPIRE! A ZOMBIE
   GHOUL!
SCARE YOUR NEIGHBOURS OUT OF THEIR
   WITS!"

Slowly my face began to change
As I carefully applied the pack,
I laughed at my face in the mirror
But an evil stranger leered back.

Long hair sprouted wild from my forehead,
My nose was half snout, half beak,
My right eye bulged angry and bloodshot
While the left crawled over my cheek.

My fangs hung low and broken,
My chin was cratered with sores,
The backs of my hands were mats of hair,
My fingers grew long, bird-like claws.

Heard my sister's key in the front door,
Heard her calling, "Anyone in?"
Took a long, last look at the thing in the glass,
Distorted and ugly as sin.

My sister was running the water,
She sang as she washed her hair,
I heard her call out as a floorboard creaked,
"Hello, is anyone there?"

And then I released my zombie howl
As I crashed through the kitchen door,
I caught sight of a ghoul in the window pane
And passed out cold on the floor.

Den to Let

To let
One self-contained
Detached den.
Accommodation is compact
Measuring one yard square.
Ideal for two eight-year-olds
Plus one small dog
Or two cats
or six gerbils.
Accommodation consists of:
One living-room
Which doubles as kitchen
Bedroom
Entrance-hall
Dining-room
Dungeon
Space capsule
Pirate boat
Covered waggon
Racing car
Palace·
Aeroplane
Junk-room
And look-out post.
Property is southward facing
And can be found
Within a short walking distance
Of the back door
At bottom of garden.
Easily found in the dark

By following the smell
Of old cabbages and tea-bags.
Convenient escape routes
Past rubbish dump
To Seager's Lane
Through hole in hedge,
Or into next door's garden;
But beware of next door's rhinoceros
Who sometimes thinks he's a poodle.
Construction is of
Sound corrugated iron
And roof doubles as shower
During rainy weather.
Being partially underground,
Den makes
A particularly effective hiding place

When in a state of war
With older sisters
Brothers
Angry neighbours
Or when you simply want to be alone.
Some repair work needed
To north wall
Where Mr Spence's foot came through
When planting turnips last Thursday.
With den go all contents
Including:
One carpet – very smelly
One teapot – cracked
One woolly penguin –
No beak and only one wing
One unopened tin
Of sultana pud
One hundred and three Beanos
Dated 1983–1985
And four Rupert annuals.
Rent is free
The only payment being
That the new occupant
Should care for the den
In the manner to which it has been accustomed
And on long Summer evenings
Heroic songs of days gone by
Should be loudly sung
So that old and glorious days
Will never be forgotten.

Are You There Moriarty?

None of my aunties
Cared much for Uncle Arthur.
Somewhere deep down
Where auntiness is bred
They thought of him as evil
And worse than that ill-mannered.
He dredged his tea out of a saucer
Through the yellow sieve of his great moustache;
Removed his boots in mixed company
And smoked a huge curved pipe
That smelled of condemned socks.
Sometimes, when contemplation took him,
He'd chuckle to himself at private
And disreputable thoughts
And gob a stream of thick brown juice
With sizzling accuracy
Into the heart of the fire.
Arthur wasn't the stuff
That aunts are made of.
But if you were under twelve
And relished blood and dirt
Uncle Arthur was magic!
He could wiggle his ears till the cows came home,
Belch thunderously at will
And produce streams of soft-boiled eggs
From either nostril.
At Christmas he came into his own:
Between the turkey and the pudding
He'd play a game of billiards
With his glass eye and a kitchen knife

Shouting, "Pot the red!"
At screaming Auntie Muriel
As the eye dropped into her lap.
For his piece de resistance
He'd remove his huge false teeth
And make them sing
God Save the King
As he tapped the rhythm out
With fervour on the spoons.
Then after dinner,
When the aunts retired to the parlour
To snooze and share their disapproving clucks,
Uncle Arthur would draw the blinds,
Turn out the lights
And tell us harrowing tales
Of headless, bloodstained men
Who flew down children's chimneys
And performed such hideous deeds
The girls had nightmares into March,
While Cousin Edgar,
Who was sensitive
And pressed wild flowers,
Wet the bed until his dying day.
When only the strong remained,
We'd play Uncle Arthur's favourite game
"Are you there Moriarty?"
Which involved a string of juvenile challengers
Lying blindfold on their stomachs
And screaming out the challenge
While trying to knock each other senseless
With rolled up copies of *The Echo*.

Now, whenever I pass the cemetery
Where Uncle Arthur long lies buried,
I think of him,
Stretched out upon a marble slab,
His great pipe pouring smoke,
Spitting thoughtfully between his socks
And laughing at us all.
And for his sake I call,
Too quiet I know for Uncle Arthur's taste,
"Are you there Moriarty?"
And it seems to me
That from far away
I hear a rolled up paper crashing down
On some unfortunate skull
And from somewhere
Deep in Death's chill parlour
Comes the kind of sound
That disapproving aunts would make
If they could ruffle their feathers.

Conversation Piece

Late again Blenkinsop?
What's the excuse this time?
Not my fault sir.
Who's fault is it then?
Grandma's sir.
Grandma's. What did she do?
She died sir.
Died?
She's seriously dead all right sir.
That makes four grandmothers this term.
And all on P.E. days Blenkinsop.
I know. It's very upsetting sir.
How many grandmothers have you got Blenkinsop?
Grandmothers sir? None sir.
None?
All dead sir.
And what about yesterday Blenkinsop?
What about yesterday sir?
You missed maths.
That was the dentist sir.
The dentist died?
No sir. My teeth sir.
You missed the test Blenkinsop.
I'd been looking forward to it too sir.
Right, line up for P.E.
Can't sir.
No such word as can't. Why can't you?
No kit sir.

Where is it?
Home sir.
What's it doing at home?
Not ironed sir.
Couldn't you iron it?
Can't do it sir.
Why not?
My hand sir.
Who usually does it?
Grandma sir.
Why couldn't she do it?
Dead sir.

Name Poem

Borg and Best and Geoffrey Boycott,
Marvellous Marvin, Little Mo,
Graham Souness, Peter Shilton,
Johan Cruyff, Sebastian Coe.

Steve Ovett and Olga Korbut,
Willie Carson, Raymond Floyd,
Kevin Keegan, Trevor Brooking,
Zola Budd, Chris Evert-Lloyd.

Joel Garner, Arnold Palmer,
Barry John, Torvill and Dean,
Nel Tarlton, Bobby Charlton,
Vivian Richards, Barry Sheene.

Navratilova, Betty Stove,
Di Stefanno, Denis Law,
Botham, Willey, Dennis Lillee,
Mohammad Ali, Garry Shaw.

Charlie Nicholas, Jack Nicklaus,
Joe Louis, Sugar Ray,
Zico, Faldo, Pelé, Falcoã,
Michael Holding, Andy Gray.

Franz Klammer, David Gower,
Sharron Davies, Terry Paine,
Whirlwind White and Giant Haystacks,
Alex Higgins the Hurricane.

Dear Examiner

Thank you so much for your questions
I've read them all carefully through
But there isn't a single one of them
That I know the answer to.

I've written my name as instructed
Put the year, the month and the day
But after I'd finished doing that
I had nothing further to say.

So I thought I'd write you a letter
Fairly informally
About what's going on in the classroom
And what it's like to be me.

Mandy has written ten pages
But it's probably frightful guff
And Angela Smythe is copying
The answers off her cuff.

Miss Quinlan is marking our homework
The clock keeps ticking away
For anyone not in this classroom
It's just another day.

Mother's buying groceries
Grandmother's drinking tea
Unemployed men doing crosswords
Or watching "Crown Court" on TV.

The drizzle has finally stopped here
The sun's just started to shine
And in a back garden in Sefton Road
A housewife hangs shirts on the line.

A class chatters by to play tennis
The cathedral clock has just pealed
A motor chugs steadily back and forth
Mowing the hockey field.

Miss Quinlan's just seen what I've written
Her face is an absolute mask
Before she collects in the papers
I have one little favour to ask.

I thought your questions were lovely
There's only myself to blame
But couldn't you give me something
For writing the date and my name?

The Secret

Down a secret path
Through a secret wood
By the side of a secret sea,
I creep on tiptoe
To a place I know
That no one can find except me, except me,
That no one can find except me.

And the soft breeze that blows
Through the briar and the rose
That I pass along my way
Seems to whisper low,
"Remember, no one must know
The secret you've learned today, today
The secret you've learned today."

Beside that beach
Where the herring gulls screech
And the long cream breakers roll,
The voice of the sea
Whispers softly to me,
"You must not tell a soul, a soul
You must not tell a soul."

But the secret I know
Seems to grow and grow
Until it weighs me down like a load,
If I don't tell someone
Before very long
I'm sure I'm going to explode, explode
I know that I'm going to explode.

Up a path from the beach
I finally reach
A valley deep and wide,
And it's here that I tell
To an old stone well
The secret I've kept hidden inside, inside
The secret I've kept hidden inside.

In that deep well's ear
Where no one will hear
I whisper secretly
And from miles away
Each word I say
Comes echoing back to me, to me
Comes echoing back to me.

And I make my well
Promise never to tell
The words whispered secretly,
And like a far away bell
Tolls the voice of the well,
"Your secret is safe with me, with me
Your secret is safe with me."

Time Child

Dandelion, dandelion,
Dandelion flower,
If I breathe upon thee
Pray tell me the hour.

Little child, little child,
Little child I pray,
Breathe but gently on me
Lest you blow the time away.